P9-AFR-958

c.1

E
BRI

Brimner, Larry Dane.

Country Bear's
surprise.

Country Bear's Surprise

Country Bear's Surprise

By Larry Dane Brimner

Illustrations by Ruth Tietjen Councell

Orchard Books
New York

Orchard Books
A division of Franklin Watts, Inc.
387 Park Avenue South
New York, NY 10016

Printed by General Offset Company, Inc.
Bound by Horowitz / Rae.
Manufactured in the United States of America.
Book design by Inga Soderberg.

10 9 8 7 6 5 4 3 2 1

The text of this book is set in 18 pt. Cochin.
The illustrations are colored pencil drawings.

Library of Congress Cataloging-in-Publication Data

Brimner, Larry Dane.
Country Bear's surprise / by Larry Dane Brimner :
illustrations by Ruth Tietjen Councell.   p.   cm.
Summary: Trying to find out why his birthday has been forgotten,
Country Bear persists in interrupting the activities of
what appears to be a secret club.
ISBN 0-531-05811-5.   ISBN 0-531-08411-6 (lib.)
(1. Bears—Fiction.   2. Birthdays—Fiction.   3. Parties—Fiction.)
I. Councell, Ruth Tietjen, ill.   II. Title.
PZ7.B75245Co   1990   [E]—dc20   90-7717   CIP   AC

For my dear, dear friend, Lois Sims
-L.D.B.

For Sarah Beth
-R.T.C.

Can't you read, Country Bear?
It says, "Members Only"!

You want to celebrate?
But there is nothing
to celebrate, Country Bear.

Peeking in the window
will do you no good, Country Bear.
This is a secret club…for members only.

You were not peeking?
You were just looking for an apple?

But this is not an apple tree, Country Bear.

Back again?
You think I have forgotten
something important?
But I know the Secret Knock.
I know the Secret Password.
And I even know the Secret Hug.

You did not mean any of those?
Well then, Country Bear, what do you mean?

Dressing up as a cake
looks like fun, Country Bear,
but Halloween is a long
time away.

Oh, it isn't for Halloween?
It is to jog my memory?
But, Country Bear, there is
nothing wrong with my memory.

You are not sure about that.
Country Bear, whatever can you mean?

TAP-TAPPETY-TAP!

Hey, Country Bear, you know the Secret Knock!
What? You are going to find someone to celebrate
your birthday with?
But "birthday" <u>is</u> the Secret Password, Country Bear.
Oh, you'd like someone to give you a bear hug?
Well, Country Bear, that <u>is</u> the Secret Hug!
Now put down your suitcase and come inside.

SURPRISE, COUNTRY BEAR!
We did not forget your birthday.
What's that?
Of course, you knew that,
Country Bear.

COUNTRY BEAR'S SURPRISE COOKIES

1 cup (2 sticks) butter, softened

½ cup granulated sugar

¼ teaspoon salt

1 large egg

1 tablespoon vanilla extract

2 cups unsifted all-purpose flour

colored sugar

In a medium-sized bowl, beat together the butter, sugar, and salt with an electric mixer until fluffy. Add the egg and vanilla, beating until well combined. Next, add the flour and beat at low speed only until the mixture forms a ball. Divide the dough in half and wrap both pieces tightly in plastic. Refrigerate for at least one hour before rolling.

While preheating the oven to 325°F, roll out the dough to ¼-inch thickness on a lightly floured surface. Cut in desired shapes with cookie cutters and place ½-inch apart on an ungreased baking sheet. Sprinkle with colored sugar. Then bake 12 to 15 minutes or until edges just start to brown. When cool, surprise someone special!
Makes about 2 dozen cookies.